This Ladybird book belongs to

Jamie Lp

aged 6 years old on

9 January

Contents

A catalogue record for this book is available from the British Library

Published by Ladybird Books Ltd
80 Strand London WC2R 0RL
A Penguin Company

2 4 6 8 10 9 7 5 3 1

© LADYBIRD BOOKS LTD MCMLXXXIX / MCMXCIV. This edition MMI
LADYBIRD and the device of a Ladybird are trademarks of Ladybird Books Ltd

Storytime for

6

year olds

by Joan Stimson
illustrated by Chloë March

Ladybird

Smart Alec

Alec was a peacock. He lived at the Better Birds Bird Park, but he never played with the other birds. He just thought about his looks all day.

Alec even owned a comb that had been dropped one day by a careless tourist.

"It would be lovely to have a mirror as well as a comb," sighed Alec. "But at least I can look at myself in the lake."

Each day Alec strutted down to the water, opened his tail wide and gazed at his reflection. "What a smart bird!" he said to himself. And got out his comb.

It drove the other birds mad. "Just look at Smart Alec," they groaned. "That peacock's a pain!"

The herons wanted Alec to play hide and seek. "Come on," said Harry. "Shut up your tail for once and play with us."

"No, thanks," said Alec. "I'm busy." He spread his tail even wider. And carried on combing.

Next came the new ducklings. "*Beep, beep, be our goalie,*" they begged. "We want to play football with the chicks. And your tail will *fill* our goal."

"All right," said Alec. "But not for long."

Alec didn't like being goalie. Every time the ball hit his tail, it flattened his feathers. He left the goal wide open, and rushed back to the lake.

Alec peered anxiously at his reflection. Whatever had those chicks done to his tail?

Alec combed his feathers all afternoon. At last he was satisfied. "Gosh!" he said. "I look smarter than ever!"

The other birds couldn't stand it any longer. "Just listen to Smart Alec," they groaned. "It's time we taught him a lesson."

7

The best bird brain at the Park was Phoebe Flamingo. Harry Heron went to see her with their problem.

"We just want Alec to forget about his looks," he said, "and behave like a normal bird."

Phoebe stood on one leg and thought deep thoughts. Then she came up with a Plan.

The first part of the Plan was to collect some banana skins. Harry passed on the message to the other birds. They set to work right away.

The birds lurked near litter bins. They grovelled in the grass. They peered in picnics. The tourists had never known them so friendly.

Alec knew nothing about Phoebe's Plan. He was too busy – combing his tail!

The next day dawned warm and clear. "I can't wait to see my reflection," cried Alec, and he rushed down to the lake as usual.

But things had changed since his last visit. The other birds had worked all night.

Wheeee! Alec slid right down the bank. It was *covered* in banana skins.

Splash! Alec fell into the lake – comb and all.

At last he came up for air. *Whatever* would he say? But Alec didn't *say* anything. He just shrieked and screamed, "That banana skin slide was fantastic. I never knew I could whizz so fast. This water feels wonderful. I must take a dip more often."

10

The other birds could hardly believe their
ears. "What about your tail, Alec?" cried
Harry Heron.

"*Beep, beep,* be careful of your feathers,"
warned the ducklings.

But Smart Alec didn't hear a word. He was
too busy splashing and diving. And he
wasn't looking for his comb either.

Alec was behaving just like any normal bird
and – *having fun!*

Just in time

"Next stop, Giraffe Junction," cried the Station Master.

Geoffrey was excited. It was his first day as an engine driver.

The Station Master shouted some tips: "Check the signal. Duck down at the Dark Tunnel. And watch out for zebras!"

WAY OUT

The passengers settled into their seats. The Station Master looked at his watch and blew his whistle. Then Geoffrey drove the train out of the station and onto the plain.

The train began to pick up speed. In the distance was a signal box. Geoffrey gave the signalman a cheery wave.

Then he remembered – to check the signal.
"Help!" cried Geoffrey. "The signal
says **STOP**."

Screeeech! He slammed on the brakes.
The train stopped just in time – to miss
the Elephant Express.

Geoffrey set off again. But the hard work was making him hungry, and he took out his sandwiches. As he swept the crumbs off his lap, he saw the sign…

DARK TUNNEL

"Help!" cried Geoffrey. "Heads down, everybody!" Everyone ducked just in time – to miss the roof of the tunnel.

The train chugged back onto the plain.
Geoffrey could just see Giraffe Junction.
He turned round to tell the passengers.
"Look out!" they shouted.
"Zebras crossing!"

"Help!" cried Geoffrey. "There's no time to
stop." So he blew his whistle at the top of
its blow.

Whoo! Whoo! went the train. *Whoosh!* went the zebras. They leapt off the rails just in time – to save their toes.

Geoffrey pulled the train into Giraffe Junction, and the Station Master opened the doors. He looked at the clock. "Phew!" said Geoffrey.

"Well done!" said the Station Master. "You're *just in time!*"

GIRAFFE JUNCTION

Mavis and the pet sitter

Amanda Bailey was a pet sitter. When friends went away, Amanda looked after rabbits, tortoises, budgies, goldfish, guinea pigs, hamsters, tadpoles; and even cats and dogs.

One day a sheep arrived on Amanda's doorstep. Her farmer trudged behind.

"Baa!" bleated the sheep.

"Wedding!" grunted Farmer Grimes.

Amanda looked puzzled. Farmer Grimes explained, "Friend's wedding. Best suit job. Mavis ain't invited."

Amanda liked the idea of looking after Mavis. There was just one problem.

"Our garden's too small, Mr Grimes," said Amanda. "Mavis needs a big field."

"Not 'er!" grunted Farmer Grimes.

"Naa!" bleated Mavis. She shook her head.

19

"Mavis ain't a *field* sheep," said Farmer Grimes. "Mavis be one of the *family*. All 'er needs is good grub, good company and a bit of fun."

"I'll do my best, Mr Grimes," said Amanda.

Farmer Grimes set off to find his best suit. Amanda and Mavis set off for the shops.

Mavis wanted to look in *all* the shop windows. Now and then she bleated with excitement.

Suddenly there was a dreadful rumbling noise. "Listen to that thunder!" said Amanda. "We're in for a storm."

But no more rain came – just more terrible rumbling noises. Mavis rubbed her tummy.

21

"I *am* sorry," said Amanda. "I guess you want your lunch."

"*Baa,*" said Mavis. She pointed to a sign:
SNACK SHACK CAFÉ – ALL TASTES CATERED FOR.

At first the café owner was shocked to see a sheep, but then he remembered his sign. He handed over the menu. "Today's special," he said, "is egg, beans and chips."

"*Baa! Baa!*" said Mavis. That was her favourite.

Amanda and Mavis felt better for their lunch.

"Next stop, the library," said Amanda.
"I need a new reading book."

"Naa!" said Mavis. She stamped her foot.
The library sounded boring. But Amanda
knew when to be firm. "You be a good girl
at the library, *then* I'll take you to the park."

"Baa," said Mavis. It was a deal.

At the library Miss Woolthorpe got very excited. They were holding an exhibition on the woollen industry, and she wanted Mavis to be a *live* exhibit.

Mavis posed quietly, while the children sketched. She allowed them to feel her coat. But then Mavis got tired of standing still. She started to slither across the polished floor.

"All right," said Amanda. "I can take a hint. There'll be a proper slide at the park."

The Park Keeper gaped when he saw Mavis. He looked carefully through his rules and regulations, but there was nothing to say that sheep shouldn't use the equipment.

25

"No funny business, mind," he warned.

"*Naa,*" said Mavis. And slid backwards down the slide.

Amanda pushed Mavis on the swings. Then she looked at her watch. "It's time to go back," she said.

Amanda hummed happily all the way back home. Then she patted Mavis. "How was that for good grub, good company and a bit of fun?" she asked.

"*Baa! Baa!*" said Mavis. She rubbed up against Amanda's legs.

Very soon Farmer Grimes arrived. Mavis didn't recognise him in his best suit. But then he gave her a hug.

"*Baa!*" bleated Mavis.

"*I'm back!*" grunted Farmer Grimes. And for the first time that day – *he smiled!*

The robot

Albert and Elsie were ants. They didn't like work. So they sent off for a robot – to do everything for them.

Albert and Elsie didn't bother to read the instructions. They assembled their robot in a hurry. His name was Ronald.

Albert pressed Ronald's START button. "*Cakes*, Ronald," said Elsie. "I want you to make us some cakes."

CLUNK, CLUNK, Ronald strode into the kitchen. CLINK, CLINK, he took out the cooking utensils. Soon he had made a dozen cakes.

"Not bad, Ronald," said Albert.

"Mmmm," said Elsie. "Cakes taste so much better when someone else has made them."

Albert and Elsie put their feet up. Ronald went on baking. He filled the kitchen with cakes. Then cakes began to appear in the living room.

"Albert!" cried Elsie. "Press Ronald's stop button."

But Ronald didn't have a *stop* button. It was still in the box.

"We'll have to wait for Ronald's batteries to wear down," said Albert.

It took a long time for Ronald's batteries to wear down. And, by then, there were cakes *everywhere*, enough to feed an army.

Suddenly, from the street, they heard the sound of marching feet – "*Left, right, left, right.*" It was a whole army of ants.

Albert rushed into the street, to speak to them. Then he rushed back to Elsie.

"Thank goodness!" cried Albert. "The army's arrived just in time and they haven't eaten yet. Come on, Elsie. Operation *carry out the cakes!*"

A circus tale

Trevor the polar bear made an announcement. "I'm going south," he said. "I want to join the circus."

"Whatever can a polar bear do in a circus?" asked his family.

"Just you wait and see," said Trevor.

The journey south was hot and tiring.

Trevor began to wonder whether he would ever get there. But at last he saw a huge tent. "It's *Fred's famous circus!*" he cried.

When Trevor introduced himself to Fred, Fred looked him up and down. "Try the high wire," he said. Trevor climbed a long ladder right up into the big top. Then he grasped the balancing pole.

FRED'S CIRCUS

"Don't look down!" cried Fred. But he was too late. Trevor had already fallen into the safety net. At last he bounced to a halt.

"Take a ride," Fred suggested. "Take a bareback ride."

Trevor nodded eagerly. Two white ponies trotted into the ring. Trevor planted one foot firmly on the back of each pony and the threesome set off. But not for long.

"*Ooh! Aah!*" groaned the ponies, and stood still. "Trevor's too heavy," they said. "We'll *never* be able to prance with a polar bear on our backs."

"Do you bears from up north cycle?" asked Fred.

Trevor beamed. "I ride forwards, backwards, one-handed and no-handed," he said, "with no trouble at all."

But there was trouble in store. The circus cycle only had one wheel. Trevor was used to a *trike*!

Fred thought hard. "The lion tamer's due to retire," he said.

Trevor looked nervous. He tiptoed up to the lion's cage and said softly, "Good morning, lions. How would you like to hear a little rhyme?"

The lions leaned forward.

"Well," began Trevor, taking a deep breath:
"There was a young tiger of Hampstead
Whose stripes turned bright blue and then red.
They faded to pink,
I really don't think,
That tiger's quite right, do you, Fred?"

"*Ho! Ho! Ho!*" The lions rolled around their cage. "That's a good one," they roared. Fred roared with laughter too. But then he frowned. "It won't work," said Fred. "The lions must be dignified at all times. That's what the public pays for."

Worse was to come…

"If Trevor can't walk the high wire, can't ride ponies, can't trick cycle and can't tame the lions, then Trevor must *sell ice cream*," said Fred.

"Oh no!" groaned Trevor. "I didn't come all this way to sell ice cream. Whatever will my family say?" He bounded off in disgust, too upset to see Colin the clown.

Crash! Trevor bumped into Colin's bucket.

Splash! Colin soaked Trevor with water.

Dash! Trevor tore round the ring with Colin – tucked under his arm.

"That's it!" cried Fred. *"Trevor's a born clown."*

Overnight Trevor became a star, and brought more fame than ever to Fred's circus.

Trevor liked being a clown. And he *loved* getting soaked.

Because, when a polar bear comes south, he needs help – *to keep cool!*